GROW KIND

By Jon Lasser, PhD
and Sage Foster-Lasser

Illustrated by
Christopher Lyles

Magination Press • Washington, DC • American Psychological Association

To Sarah (Bubby/Bubs)—*JL*

To Ramona (Moni)—*SF-L*

For my mother, who has given me
endless amounts of love, support, and
encouragement along the way.—*CL*

Magination Press
Books for Kids From the
American Psychological Association

Copyright © 2020 by Magination Press, an imprint of the
American Psychological Association. Illustrations copyright
© 2020 by Christopher Lyles. All rights reserved. Except as
permitted under the United States Copyright Act of 1976, no
part of this publication may be reproduced or distributed in
any form or by any means, or stored in a database or retrieval
system, without the prior written permission of the publisher.
Magination Press is a registered trademark of the American
Psychological Association. Order books at maginationpress.
org, or call 1-800-374-2721.

Book design by Gwen Grafft

Printed by Worzalla, Stevens Point, WI

Library of Congress Cataloging-in-Publication Data

Names: Lasser, Jon (Psychology professor), author. |
  Foster-Lasser, Sage, author. | Lyles, Christopher,
  1977- illustrator.
Title: Grow kind / by Jon Lasser and Sage Foster-Lasser ;
  illustrated by Christopher Lyles.
Description: Washington DC : Magination Press, [2020] |
  "American Psychological Association." | Summary: Young
  Kiko, aided by her teenaged sister, Annie, and her dog,
  Chico, grows kind as they harvest fruits, flowers, and
  vegetables from their garden and share them with others.
  Includes note for parents and caregivers.
Identifiers: LCCN 2019009864| ISBN 9781433830501
  (hardcover) | ISBN 1433830507 (hardcover)
Subjects: | CYAC: Kindness—Fiction. | Gardening—
  Fiction. | Sisters—Fiction. | Dogs—Fiction.
Classification: LCC PZ7.1.L375 Gv 2020 | DDC [E]—dc23
LC record available at https://lccn.loc.gov/2019009864

Manufactured in the United States of America
10 9 8 7 6 5 4 3 2 1

My name is Kiko. I grow kind.
I will show you how, but first, I have a question for you.

Who helps you
wake up in the morning?

This morning, Chico
woke me up by licking
my face. We went outside
to check the garden.

We saw peas and peaches, tomatoes and potatoes, radishes and roses, blackberries and broccoli, melons and marigolds, and so much more!

I wanted to wake up Annie,
but Mom and Dad stopped me.

"Be kind to Annie and let her rest," said
Mom. "Teenagers need a lot of sleep."

I really wanted to show Annie everything
growing in the garden, but I played fetch with
Chico outside and waited for her to wake up.

Finally, Annie woke up.
"You're up, you're up!"
I grabbed Annie's hand and
pulled her toward the garden.

"Beautiful!" Annie said. "I know you worked hard caring for your garden. Do you need help to harvest?"

Annie and I filled our arms with lots of yummy
fruits and vegetables and some pretty flowers.

I gave spinach, carrots, peppers, and
broccoli to my dad because he likes to cook.
"Wonderful!" he said. "Thank you!"

The gift of veggies made my dad so happy. I wanted to share with other people, too. Annie and I loaded up the wagon with food and flowers.

"Being kind to our friends and neighbors helps them feel good," I told Annie.

"And it helps you feel good, too!" said Annie.

We pulled the heavy wagon down
our street, delivering delicious gifts.

Blackberries for Keisha, who loves sweet fruit.

Soft, ripe tomatoes for Ms. Stevens, who has a hard time chewing.

Peppers and corn for our next-door neighbors,
Matt and Mitch, who love to grill.

Potatoes for Dr. Thompson, who makes fresh potato salad.

Sunflowers for Mr. Carrol, who needs cheering up.

When we got to Mr. Carrol's house, we slowly
walked to the front door. I was nervous. One time,
he shouted at Chico for running into his yard.

But when Mr. Carrol opened the door, a smile lit
up his face. "Thank you both," he said. "You're
very kind." He gave Chico a gentle pat on the head.

The next day, I packed a box full of fruits and vegetables
to share with my teacher and friends at school.

But on the drive to school, I saw someone standing
on the corner. I asked my mom if we could stop.

I opened up the box. "What do you like to eat?" I asked.

"Those peaches look delicious," she replied.

I gave her some, and she waved as we said goodbye.

During show and tell,
I listened carefully
to my friends.

Ida brought her pet turtle.

Don brought
a jigsaw puzzle.

Carmen brought her
watercolor painting.

When it was my turn, I said,
"I brought my garden!"
I gave everyone something to eat.
"It's show and tell and share!"
It made me feel so good to see
everyone enjoying their fresh snacks.

That night, I took out my journal to write about my day.
I wrote about Mr. Carrol's smile, peaches for a hungry woman,
my friends enjoying the garden's fruits, and Annie's helpful ways.
Taking time to be kind to others makes everyone feel good.

Growing a garden and sharing
the harvest helped me grow kind.

How do you grow kind?

Note to Parents and Other Caregivers

Books help us understand our experiences, connect to the thoughts and feelings of others, and show us possibilities. When we read picture books like *Grow Kind* to children, we create the opportunity to explore the social and emotional skills that children need to develop for success at home, school, and in communities. There are many areas of social emotional learning, including self-awareness and self-management. In *Grow Kind*, the focus is on social awareness and relationship skills.

Young children often put themselves first, and this egocentrism is a normal part of early childhood. The ability to think about how our behaviors affect others develops gradually during early childhood, so young children may be seen as both self-absorbed and increasingly empathic as they mature. Many parents notice early childhood behaviors such as grabbing toys from others and shouting "Mine!" While these behaviors may not seem very kind, adults must remember that the capacity to share and show kindness slowly develops over time. Empathy can be seen in toddlers and becomes more pronounced with maturation, particularly as children develop greater capacities in the areas of language, cognition, and social skills.

As children's brains develop, so does their ability to see things from the perspective of others. Kindness requires some thought about the needs and feelings of others. Just as kids develop better motor skills through activity and practice, social skills increase when children observe, think about, and engage in social activity. For kindness to grow, children need to see it in their own lives and have opportunities to demonstrate kind behaviors.

How to Use This Book

Kiko's parents encourage her to take her sister's perspective by asking her to let her sister get some much needed sleep. Later, Kiko thinks about her neighbors' preferences and needs. These examples model the idea of taking another person's point of view. When reading *Grow Kind* to children, ask them about the thoughts and feelings of characters in the book to help them with perspective-taking. For example, "How did the woman on the corner feel when Kiko gave her some food?"

When children act in ways that are not kind, what's the best way for adults to respond? It may be helpful to communicate concern about the person who was harmed. For example, "When you threw that block at Matthew he looked scared. Let's go check on him to see if he's ok." This response will likely be more helpful than punishing the block thrower, because expressing concern for the other child facilitates perspective-taking and provides an opportunity to heal the relationship. It may also be helpful for adults to work with kids to identify the underlying feeling or concern that contributed to the behavior. Perhaps an unmet need can be addressed to prevent further harm.

Ultimately, we must make sure that we have developmentally appropriate expectations for young children. In early childhood, self-regulation and social skills are still developing, so the best way to help kids grow kind is to patiently support their acquisition of these important skills in a positive way. By reading *Grow Kind* with children, you're providing examples of how children can be generous with others and show kindness across social settings.

How to Help Your Child

In the book, Kiko cultivates kindness through different experiences. The scenarios described in Kiko's story are common for many young children. Here we provide some specific examples of how you can help your child grow kind using Kiko's methods.

Identify Kindness When You See It

If your child engages in an act of kindness towards a sibling, friend, or adult, recognize the act and encourage them to think about it. For example, "You shared your truck with Maggie. How kind of you to give her a turn." In addition, try to identify and discuss acts of kindness directed towards your child or yourself. For example, if a sibling helps your child with their homework, you might help your child to view and appreciate that help as an act of kindness. Say something like, "Maria is kind to help you with your math homework. She must really love you."

Talk About How Kindness Makes People Feel

Ask your child questions such as, "How do you think Maggie felt after you offered her your truck to play with?" You can help your child with this process by talking about your own emotional responses to kindness. For example, "When my friend does something kind for me, I feel happy. It makes me feel like she cares about me, and makes me feel good inside." Ask your child to describe how instances of kindness make them feel as you observe them in everyday life. This will help them become more attuned to their own feelings and the feelings of others.

Engage in Play That Teaches Kindness

Integrate kindness into playtime! Encourage your child to make decisions in play that reflect positive interpersonal relationships. For example, "Wow, that food you're making looks so delicious! Do you think your neighbor might like some?" If a character is sad or upset in the game, ask your child what someone else could do to make them feel better. This can direct the play in such a way that your child gains experience engaging in acts of kindness from a variety of perspectives.

Address the Importance of Self-Compassion

An aspect of kindness that is sometimes overlooked is kindness towards oneself. Try identifying the need for self-care and kindness when it arises. If your child is feeling poorly and can't make it to a birthday party, you might say, "I know Sara will miss having you at her party, but sometimes you have to take care of yourself. You're being kind to yourself by allowing yourself to get the rest you need." If your child is engaging in self-critical behavior, point out that they ought to be kinder to themselves. For example, "I notice that you're not very happy with the drawing you made. Sometimes, we are less kind to ourselves than we are to others. Instead of talking about what you don't like about it, let's think of three things about it that you do like."

Resources

Magination Press Family
maginationpressfamily.com

The Collaborative for Academic, Social, and Emotional Learning (CASEL)
casel.org

Social Emotional Learning Collection
rif.org/literacy-central/collections/rif-and-magination-press-social-emotional-learning-collection

Miller, P. Z. (2018). *Be Kind*. New York, NY: Roaring Brook Press

---

About the Authors
Jon Lasser is a school psychologist and Associate Dean of Research in the College of Education at Texas State University in San Marcos. He lives in Martindale, TX. Visit him on Twitter @jonslasser. This is the third book in this series he has co-authored with his daughter, **Sage Foster-Lasser**. Sage earned her bachelor's degree at the University of Texas at Austin, where she studied psychology and American studies.

About the Illustrator
Christopher Lyles is an illustrator, designer, and art educator. His work has been featured in magazines, greeting cards, and children's books, including *Grow Happy* and *Grow Grateful*. He lives in Connecticut with his wife and two kids. Visit chrislylesdesigns.com and follow him on Facebook @Chris Lyles Designs, Twitter @ChrisLyles, and Instagram @ChrisLyles.

About Magination Press
Magination Press is an imprint of the American Psychological Association. Our books for young readers make navigating life's challenges a little easier. Visit maginationpress.org or on facebook and twitter @MaginationPress.